To Whom the Angel Spoke

This story was originally dedicated to my grandsons, Brooks and Jordan. Since its publication in 1991, the family has grown. Therefore in this edition, I happily add the names of my other grandchildren, Cheyenne, Tommie, Winn, Casual, Brandon, and Wyatt, and of my step-grandchildren, Beverly and Christopher. And with great joy, I introduce my great-grandchildren, Breeana and Madison.

With my love,

Papa

Published by
PEACHTREE PUBLISHERS
1700 Chattahoochee Avenue
Atlanta, Georgia 30318-2112

Text © 2009 by Terry Kay
Illustrations © 1991, 2009 by Eileen Blyth

Illustrations created in acrylic on paper. Text typeset in Locarno Light; title and initial capitals typeset in Papyrus.
Composition and design by Regina Dalton-Fischel.

Printed and bound in China
10 9 8 7 6 5 4 3 2 1
Second Edition

Cataloging-in-Publication Data
Kay, Terry.
  To whom the angel spoke : a story of the Christmas / written by Terry Kay ; illustrated by Eileen Blyth. -- 2nd ed.
    p. cm.
  ISBN 978-1-56145-502-7 / 1-56145-502-4
  1. Jesus Christ--Nativity--Juvenile literature. 2. Shepherds in the Bible--Juvenile literature.. I. Blyth, Eileen. II. Title.
  BT315.3.K39 2009
  232.92'2--dc22
                              2009003588

To Whom the Angel Spoke

Angel Spoke

A Story of the Christmas

Written by
Terry Kay

Illustrated by
Eileen Blyth

PEACHTREE
ATLANTA

Once, there were three shepherds who lived together while keeping watch over their sheep.

Oh, there might have been more than three of them, but that doesn't matter. Three is a good number. Not too few. Not too many.

What does matter is that the three shepherds were good at their work, and their work was not easy. They had to protect their flocks from wild animals, and they had to know where to find fields of deep, thick grass and pools of clean, clear water. They had to know when their sheep were restless and wanted to move about, or when they wanted to rest.

Certainly, the three shepherds knew about sheep.

Still, as people living together, they were different, as all people everywhere are different.

One shepherd was tall.

Another shepherd was short.

The third shepherd was neither tall nor short. He looked short when he stood beside the tall shepherd and tall when he stood beside the short shepherd.

He was in-between. Medium.

* * *

One shepherd was fat.

Another shepherd was thin.

The third shepherd was neither fat nor thin. He looked fat when he stood beside the thin shepherd and thin when he stood beside the fat shepherd.

He was in-between. Medium.

One shepherd was black.

Another shepherd was white.

The third shepherd was neither black nor white. His skin was the color of rich bronze. When he stood beside the black shepherd, he looked curiously pale, but when he stood beside the white shepherd, he looked curiously dark. It was even more curious how he looked when he stood beside both his friends at the same time——a kind of pale-dark, dark-pale.

You see, he was——well, in-between. Medium.

The three shepherds were different, as all people, everywhere, are different.

Because they were shepherds, they would spend much of their time sitting and relaxing, watching as their sheep huddled in twos and threes and fours to graze, and they would listen to the wind as it dipped and soared through the hills.

One shepherd said the wind made him lonely. He thought a man should have a home and not wander like a nomad through the hills. "A person should have a place to go to at nighttime," he said. "He should have a bed, a warm bed, on cold nights."

Another shepherd said the wind made him restless. He thought he should have been a world traveler.

"Ah, that would have been a wonderful life," he said dreamily. "To travel the great roads, to meet great people in great places."

The third shepherd—the in-between, medium
one—said he didn´t really think about the wind.
It was part of being a shepherd and, after all, that´s
what he was—a shepherd.

The only thing the third shepherd was curious about was the constant caravan of people going into the small town of Bethlehem to pay a tax to the king named Herod.

"I did not know so many had moved away," he said quietly. "I wonder if any of them are old friends. Perhaps I played with some of them as a boy." He smiled softly and added, "I remember playing hide-and-seek. I could hide in such places that no one could find me."

One of the other shepherds laughed. "So that's where your sheep learned their hiding tricks," he said.

And, so, the three men who were shepherds sat
on the top of a hill overlooking Bethlehem and
watched the faraway, thin line of people moving
slowly along a rough, dusty road toward the town.

Everyone who lived back then——back in the time of the three shepherds—— remembered the night.

Sunset opened in a splatter of color——orange and red and purple. Slender streams of light reaching out from the palm of the sun, reaching out high and long to catch something in their bright fingers. Trees. Hills. The buildings of Bethlehem. Something. Anything.

The three shepherds marveled at the sunset. They stood, side by side——the in-between shepherd standing between the tall shepherd and the short shepherd——and they cupped their hands over their eyes to shade out the glare. The light settled over them and threw their shadows——tall, in-between, short shadows——against the mountains.

"Beautiful!" said one shepherd.

"Magnificent!" said another shepherd.

"Wonderful!" said the third shepherd.

For one rare moment, the three had agreed on something.

Even the sheep, which usually had little concern for such things, looked at the sunset. Some of them bleated. All of them looked.

And then the sunset disappeared and stars began to pop out against the blot of darkness. The stars sparkled and flamed and seemed to dance with gladness.

"I see bad weather in this night," said one of the shepherds, as he prepared to raise a tent.

"As usual, you are wrong," said another shepherd. "I think it is a good omen. I think we will have days of good grazing, valleys of thick grass and flowing streams of water."

"I do not know," said the third shepherd. "If it is not one, perhaps it will be the other."

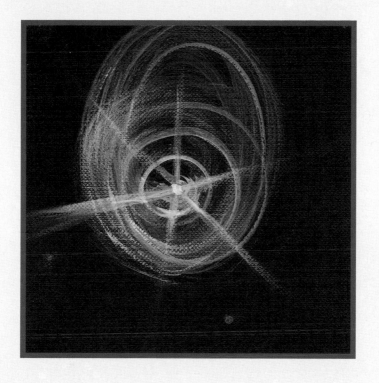

"I think this is strange," said the black shepherd—
or it might have been the white shepherd, or even
the bronze shepherd; anyway, one of them said it:
"I think above us is the brightest star the heavens
ever held."

His friends nodded.

"Yes," said one.

"Quite so," said the other.

Again, the three shepherds had agreed on something.

* * *

The star above them glittered like a brilliant, giant jewel turning with the wind. It caught the glow of the moon and the other stars and threw the light toward earth, toward Bethlehem.

The three shepherds whispered in awe, each saying
the same thing:

"Look . . ."

"Look . . ."

"Look . . ."

And as they were watching the star pour down its golden light upon Bethlehem and the hills around Bethlehem, the three shepherds heard something that sounded like a Voice—words from the throat of the wind—rushing up from a distant valley, sliding over the lap of the hills in a whistling cry like the gathering of a sudden storm.

"What was that?" cried one of the shepherds.

"A voice," muttered the second shepherd. "A...a windvoice."

"Yes, I heard it, too," whispered the third shepherd. "It—it said something like—like, 'Fear not...'"

"Yes, yes, that was it," the first shepherd agreed.
"'Fear not.' But why am I so afraid?"

The three shepherds moved closer together,
huddling like their sheep.

Again, they heard the rushing sound of the Windvoice, mightier than before, and the light of the star rolled over them. They fell to the ground, pulling their cloaks over their faces, trying to hide from the light and the Windvoice.

And then the Windvoice became loud and clear. It said again: *"Fear not ..."*

"... for, behold, I bring you good tidings of great joy, which shall be to all people ..."

The three shepherds hugged each other in fear.

"Oh, what is happening?" they cried, trembling so hard they were bumping heads.

And again the Voice surrounded them:

"For unto you is born this day in the City of
David, a Saviour, which is Christ the Lord.
And this shall be a sign unto you: Ye shall find
the Babe wrapped in swaddling clothes, lying in
a manger."

Then, out of the heavens, the shepherds heard
other voices—voices that exploded and echoed
throughout the hills:

"Glory to God in the highest, and on earth peace, good will toward men."

And then the voices were gone, leaving a silence as still as morning, untouched and clean. The three shepherds pulled their cloaks from over their faces and looked at one another.

"How could this be?" whispered one.

"I do not know," said another. "How can voices come out of the wind? Does the wind know how to speak?"

"But it did," said the third. "It was the voice of God. It had to be. Did we not hear the words?"

The other shepherds agreed.

"Yes . . ."

"Yes . . ."

The three shepherds stared at the star burning in the sky above them.

"It brings all the light of the other stars to it," said the tall shepherd.

"I think it is the sun, which has broken apart," guessed the short shepherd.

"But why did its light fall on us?" asked the in-between shepherd.

Then one of them said, "Let us go now even unto Bethlehem, and see this thing which is come to pass, which the Lord hath made known unto us."

"Yes, I agree," said another of the shepherds.

"Yes, let us go," said the third shepherd.

And, so, the three shepherds went into Bethlehem, following the bright path of the brightest star above them, and they came to a place where the child who would be named Jesus lay, wrapped in swaddling clothes as the Windvoice had promised.

One by one, they bowed quietly before the child, and then each went away to tell a different story of what had happened, because the three shepherds —those to whom the angel spoke—were different, as all people, everywhere, are different.

Yet, they heard a Voice one night, and because they believed what the Voice told them, they were alike.

And again that Voice speaks. To all who are different, but are seekers and askers and believers, that Voice is heard always at the Christmas. It says—as it said to the three shepherds:

"For unto you is born this day in the City of
David, a Saviour, which is Christ the Lord . . ."

Amen. Amen.

Author's Note

I wrote the first version of this story many years ago as a reading on invitation from a church to create a Christmas program. It remained that—a reading—until Peachtree Publishers offered it in publication. I love the book and am grateful to have it in my collection of writings, yet I still think of it first as a reading, something to be said aloud, because I believe there are some stories that beg to be declared in voice. The birth of Christ is one of them for me.

In this version I have elected to use scripture found in the Book of Luke from the King James version of the Bible. It is a personal preference, having absolutely nothing to do with theology, but everything to do with poetry.

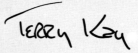